# Grandmama's Joy

BY ELOISE GREENFIELD  Illustrated by Carole Byard

PHILOMEL BOOKS
New York

Philomel Books, a division of
The Putnam & Grosset Group,
200 Madison Avenue, New York, N.Y. 10016.

Library of Congress Cataloging in Publication Data
Greenfield, Eloise.   Grandmama's joy.
Summary: A little girl tries to cheer up her despondent
grandmother by reminding her of some very important things.
[1. Grandmothers—Fiction]    I. Byard, Carole M.    II. Title.
PZ7.G84Gr    [Fic]    79-11403
ISBN 0-399-21064-4
13   15   14

# Grandmama's Joy

*For Raymond, Andrea, Wendell and Pam*

Her grandmama was sad and Rhondy didn't know why. It wasn't one of those rainy, gray days that sometimes made Grandmama so quiet. It was a gold and blue day. People were taking their time going places in the sunshine, and Rhondy could see all the way to the high school.

But still, Grandmama was sad, taking old clothes out of the closet and stuffing them into a big box.

Rhondy knew just what to do to make her laugh. She went to her room and put on the long earrings Mrs. Bennett had given her to play with, and she tied the plaid tablecloth with the burn hole in it around her waist. Then she rolled up a piece of newspaper and took it with her to Grandmama's room. But she didn't go in, she peeped around the door.

"Sit down, Grandmama," she said. "I got a surprise for you."

"Oh, honey!" Grandmama said with a sigh in her voice. "Grandmama doesn't have time for a show today."

"It's just a little show," Rhondy said. "It won't take but a minute. Pleeease?" She took her grandmama's arm and pulled her toward the bed and made her sit down.

"Well, all right," Grandmama said, trying to smile.

Rhondy put her newspaper-microphone up to her mouth and began to sing. She shook her shoulders and her head, and walked up and down the way she had seen singers do on television, and she

finished with her eyes closed and one arm stuck up and out.

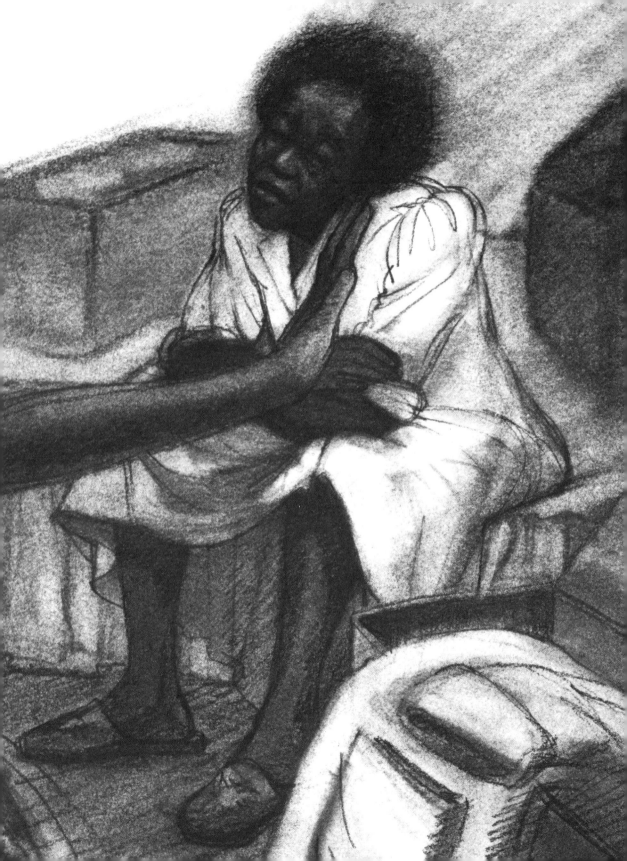

But Grandmama wasn't a good audience today. She laughed and clapped, but it wasn't a real laugh because the lines between her eyebrows never went away, and when Rhondy started out of the room and turned back to look, Grandmama was still sitting on the bed with a faraway look in her eyes.

By the time Rhondy had put her newspaper away and taken off her earrings and her tablecloth, Grandmama was cleaning out the closet again.

"I'm going outside, Grandmama," Rhondy said.

"All right," Grandmama answered. "But don't go away, now."

Rhondy walked down the street to the house with the baby rosebush beside the porch, and rang the bell. She could hear Mrs. Bennett's footsteps coming fast toward the door. Mrs. Bennett hurried everywhere, even when she wasn't in a hurry.

"Come on in," she said, pulling Rhondy inside. "Me and Tippy was just watching the ball game."

Tippy meowed and rubbed his fur against Rhondy's leg, but she didn't have time to pick him up right then. "Mrs. Bennett," she said, "can you call up my grandmama?"

"Melissa ain't sick, is she?" Mrs. Bennett asked, rushing to the phone.

"No, she's just sad," Rhondy said.

"Oh." Mrs. Bennett stood still for a moment with her hand on the phone. Then she dialed and held the phone to her ear for a long time before she hung up.

"I guess she don't feel like talking right now, Rhondy," Mrs. Bennett said. "But I'll call her again later on, hear?"

"Do you know why she's sad?" Rhondy asked.

Mrs. Bennett nodded her head. "Your grandmama's going to tell you all about it," she said. "But don't you worry now, everything's going to be all right." She and Tippy walked Rhondy to the door.

Rhondy went out the back door and walked slowly down the alley to her back yard. It was still a gold and blue day, but it didn't matter. It didn't matter that the sun was shining if it didn't make her grandmama happy. She looked around in the yard for something pretty. Grandmama liked pretty things.

Rhondy looked for a feather, or a buttercup, or a little twig with bumps on it. Then, over near the zinnias that she had helped to plant, she saw a little black stone with sparkly silver specks in it, and she picked it up and took it in the house. She found her grandmama in the kitchen drinking a cup of peppermint tea.

"I got something pretty for you, Grandmama!" she said. "It sparkles if you put it in the sun!"

Her grandmama held the stone in her hand. "Where'd you get such a pretty stone?" she asked.

"I got it in our yard," Rhondy said. "There's a whole lot of pretty things in our yard."

Grandmama made a short, jerky humming sound and looked quickly down into her cup. She drew her face together tight, but she couldn't hold it. She laid the stone on the table and started to cry.

Rhondy didn't know what to do. *She* was the one who usually cried, and Grandmama always knew what to do. But she had never seen Grandmama cry before, not *really* cry, with hard sounds and tears that left her eyes. So Rhondy just stood there, a little bit scared and wanting to cry, too, until Grandmama got quiet and reached for a paper napkin to wipe her face.

"We have to leave our yard, Rhondy," Grandmama said, crumpling the napkin in her lap. "We have to move. The rent here is too much for me now. I had to find us another place to live."

"Is it far?" Rhondy asked, thinking about missing her friends. But Grandmama didn't hear her.

"I've been living in this house for a long time, since way back, long before you were born, and now. . ." She stopped talking and looked past Rhondy's head at a way back time.

Rhondy could smell the peppermint from the teacup and feel the good kitchen feelings. She didn't want to live in another house, either. And she didn't want to leave her friends and her school and Mrs. Bennett and Tippy, and move to some place that might be far away. But she wasn't as worried as Grandmama was. Her grandmama had forgotten something, and Rhondy had to make her remember.

"Grandmama," she said, "tell me about when I came to live with you."

Grandmama shook her head. "Not right now," she said.

"Pleeease?" Rhondy said. "I'll help you." She leaned on the table close to Grandmama. "It was a rainy, gray day..."

Grandmama took a long breath in and out. "It was a rainy, gray day," she said finally, "and your mama and daddy went for a ride in the car."

"I was just a little baby," Rhondy said. "And I was in my car bed in the back seat. And then, the car slipped because the street was wet."

Rhondy saw her grandmama shiver and take another long breath, so she said the hard part fast. "And the car ran into a tree, and the policeman came and told you that Mama and Daddy had died. But I was in the hospital, and all I had was a tiny, bitty scratch on my face."

Grandmama nodded. "I went to the hospital to get you," she said, "and you were lying in that white crib, and I couldn't hardly see you for the tears in my eyes. But you saw your grandmama, and you started kicking up a storm, trying so hard to talk, and I picked you up and just held you."

Rhondy leaned in closer because now they were getting to the best part.

"And I said to myself," Grandmama said, "'that's my joy, that's Grandmama's joy. Long as I got my joy, I'll be all right.'"

Rhondy waited for Grandmama to smile. She always smiled after she said the best part, but this time she didn't look as if she had heard herself say it.

Now Rhondy was worried. She touched her grandmama's arm. "Grandmama?" she said. "Am I still your joy?"

"Oh honey, yes!" Grandmama said. She kissed Rhondy's cheek.

"Will I still be your joy when we move?"

Grandmama looked at her then, really looked at her, as if she hadn't seen her for a long time and was so glad to see her. Then she hugged her, and put Rhondy's head on her shoulder and patted her head and hugged her again. "You'll always be my joy," she said.

Rhondy didn't have to lift her head and look at Grandmama's face to know that she was smiling a real smile and that the lines between her eyebrows had gone away. Besides, Rhondy didn't want to lift her head. She liked it right where it was. She felt so happy in her grandmama's arms because as much as she was Grandmama's joy, Grandmama was her joy, too.

She squeezed her eyes shut and hugged her grandmama tight.